THE WORST TEAM EVER

WRITTEN AND ILLUSTRATED BY
LEONARD KESSLER

A YOUNG YEARLING BOOK

Published by
Dell Publishing
a division of
Bantam Doubleday Dell Publishing Group, Inc.
666 Fifth Avenue
New York, New York 10103

Reprinted by arrangement with William Morrow & Company, Inc., on behalf of Greenwillow Books

ISBN: 0-440-40428-2

Printed in the United States of America

March 1991

10 9 8 7 6 5 4 3 2 1

WES

BEFORE BASEBALL,
BEFORE SOFTBALL,
THERE WAS

SWAMPBALL

SWAMPBALL IS PLAYED WITH

A FLAT BAT

AND A ROUND BALL.

THERE ARE SIX PLAYERS ON A TEAM.

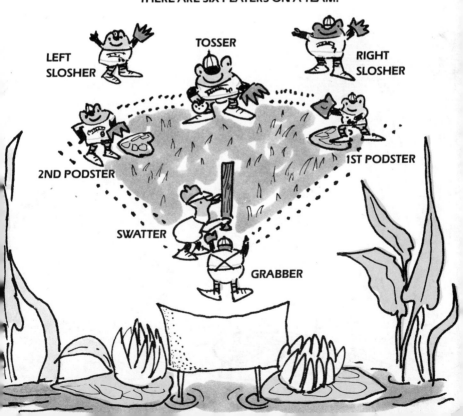

LEFT
SLOSHER

TOSSER

RIGHT
SLOSHER

2ND PODSTER

1ST PODSTER

SWATTER

GRABBER

CONTENTS

1. READ ALL ABOUT IT

"Look at this,"
said Melvin Moose.

Bobo Bullfrog and Pickles Frog

read the sports page.

"It says that our team

is the worst swampball team ever,"

said Pickles.

"We lost 35 games in a row,"

said Bobo Bullfrog.

7

"Maybe you need a new coach,"
said Melvin.

"We don't have a coach,"
said Bobo.
"The last one quit,"
said Pickles.

"That is a job for Old Turtle,"
said Melvin. "He once won
the coach of the year prize."
"Here comes Old Turtle now.
Ask him. Ask him," said Pickles.

"Hi, Old Turtle," said Melvin.

"The Green Hoppers need a new coach.
Do you want the job?"

"The Green Hoppers?" said Old Turtle.

"They lost 35 games in a row.
Get another coach."

"We need a good coach," said Bobo.

"You are the only one who can do it.

They need you," said Melvin Moose.

Old Turtle smiled.

"There is only one more game,"

said Pickles.

"We want to win that last game,"

said Bobo.

"I will coach the Green Hoppers
if Melvin will be my helper,"
said Old Turtle.
"I will help you," said Melvin.

MEET THE COACHES

"Where are the Green Hoppers?"
asked Old Turtle.
"They must be warming up,"
said Bobo.

"Green Hoppers," called Melvin.

"Come and meet

   your new head coach."

"We are over here," said Dusty Toad.

"We are resting," said the Green Hoppers.

"We always rest before we warm up,"
said Dusty.

"Everybody up," shouted Old Turtle.

"We are going to hop, jump, and slosh."

"And work on swatting and catching,"
 said Melvin.

The Green Hoppers hopped
and jumped. They sloshed
around the swampy field.
They huffed and puffed.
"We need a rest," called Dusty Toad.

"Not now," shouted Old Turtle.

"Keep hopping."

"Old Turtle will get you in shape,"
Melvin told them.

"Is it rest time yet?"
huffed the Green Hoppers.
"No, it is swatting time,"
said Old Turtle.

"I need work on my swatting.
I always hit little pop-ups,"
said Pickles. "I want to hit
whopper ploppers."
"We will help you," said Melvin.

All that day the Green Hoppers
swatted the ball.
"Time to rest now," said Old Turtle.
The team plopped down
on the ground.

Old Turtle wrote on the board:

TO BE WINNERS
YOU MUST...
1. Be in good Shape.
2. Practice. Practice.
3. Want to
        Win!

"We want to win," said Pickles.

"We want to be winners,"

the Green Hoppers cheered.

"Then you must work hard.

Be here early tomorrow,"

Old Turtle said.

3. THE TEAM SHAPES UP

"Everybody is here,"
said Old Turtle.
"Good," said Melvin.
"We'll begin with a warm-up."

"Swatting practice time,"
called Old Turtle.
"Who has the bats?"

"Bobo has the bats," said Pickles.
"Oh! Oh! I knew I forgot
something," said Bobo.

"We won't have
swatting practice today,"
said Old Turtle.
"It is hop, jump, and slosh
all day."

It was a long day
for the Green Hoppers.
Just before dark, Old Turtle said,
"That is it for today."
He wrote on the board:

1. Practice. Practice.
2. Pickles – work
   on swatting.
3. Bobo– Remember
   to bring
         BATS!!

"What is the magic word for
tomorrow?" Old Turtle asked Bobo.
"Bats," said Bobo.

The next day Bobo was the
first player on the field.
"Did you bring the bats?"
asked Old Turtle.
"I have the bats," said Bobo.

"Meet Sally and Billy Bat.

They are our bat girl and bat boy,"

he said.

"Very funny," said Old Turtle.

"Stop fooling around."

"I was only joking," said Bobo.

"Here are the swampball bats."

Old Turtle worked all week

with the Green Hoppers.

"Keep your eye on the ball,"

he told Pickles.

WHAM!

Pickles hit

a long whopper plopper.

"That is the way to hit,"

said Old Turtle.

"No more pop-ups for Pickles."

It was dark when the Green Hoppers

slowly left the field.

"Maybe we are working them

too hard," said Melvin.

"Tomorrow is the big game.

How can they be winners

if they don't work hard?"

Old Turtle asked.

4. THE LAST BIG GAME

The Green Hoppers came
to the swamp park early.
"Time to warm up,"
said Pickles.
"We can put our caps on
that new hat rack,"
said Bobo.

"Where is Melvin?" asked Old Turtle.

"He is not here yet," said Bobo.

"Maybe he quit," the Mallards shouted.

"Melvin Moose is not a quitter,"
  Old Turtle yelled back.

"Time to play," the Mallards called.

"We are waiting for Melvin Moose,"
said Pickles.

"The Green Hoppers don't want
    to play," shouted the Mallard Ducks.
"They don't want to lose
    the last game of the year!"
    yelled the Mallard captain.

"We can't wait for Melvin,"
said Old Turtle.
"Get your caps. Let's play!"
"Look. That hat rack is moving,"
shouted Bobo.
"That is not a hat rack,"
said Old Turtle.

"IT'S MELVIN MOOSE!"

they all yelled.

"I told you Melvin

is not a quitter,"

said Old Turtle.

"I slept here last night.

I did not want to be late,"

said Melvin.

"Swatter up,"

said Umpire Pelican.

The Green Hoppers hopped

out onto the field.

"Green Hoppers, you can do it!"

Old Turtle called.

5. PICKLES UP AT BAT

"It is a very close game," said Melvin.
In the last of the sixth inning
the score was tied.

	1	2	3	4	5	6	RUNS	HITS	ERRORS
MALLARD DUCKS	0	0	1	0	0	0			
GREEN HOPPERS	0	0	0	0	1				

"Bobo is on base. We need
just one hit," said Old Turtle.
"Who is the next swatter?"
asked Old Turtle.
"It is Pickles," said Melvin.

The Mallard Ducks laughed.

"Pop-up. Pop-up.

Pickles is a POP-UP,"

they all sang.

Pickles stepped into the swatter's box.

The ball zoomed over the plate.

SWISH!

He swung late and fell down.

"Time out," called Old Turtle.
Pickles stepped out of
the swatter's box.
Old Turtle whispered,
"Remember what you learned.
Keep your eye on the ball.
You will get a hit."
Pickles smiled.

The Mallard tosser was ready.

"Easy out. Easy out," he shouted.

"Not this time," said Pickles softly.

The tosser threw a fast ball

right over the plate.

POW! WHAM!

Pickles hit the ball.

Up and up it went,

over the right slosher's head.

"It is a super duper

whopper plopper!"

yelled Melvin.

Bobo and Pickles sloshed across
swamp plate.
"The Green Hoppers
are the winners!"
Old Turtle shouted.

"Old Turtle, you did it.

You are the best coach ever,"

roared Melvin.

Old Turtle smiled.

"We both helped them win,"

he said.

"But it's the team I'm proud of,"

Old Turtle said.

"You all worked hard.

You did it.

YOU WON THE GAME."

"And next year we won't be
the worst team ever," said Bobo.
"Will you be our coach
next year?" asked Pickles.
"How can I quit
when you are
on a winning streak?"
said Old Turtle.

"Watch out for the Green Hoppers

next year!" Melvin called.

"What is the magic word?"

he asked.

"OLD TURTLE!"

the Green Hoppers cheered.

A long time ago,
Old Turtle's grandfather
invented swampball.
Leonard Kessler learned
about the game by watching
Old Turtle and the Green Hoppers
play in the swamps behind his house
in Rockland County, New York.

When he is not cheering
for his favorite teams, the Green Hoppers
and the New York Mets,
Leonard Kessler is playing tennis.